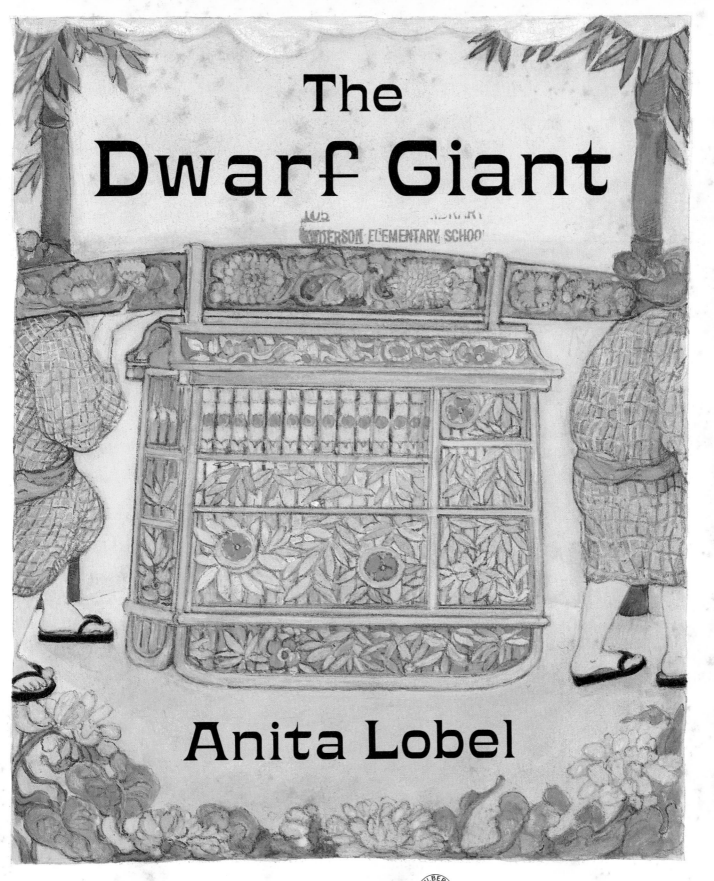

The
Dwarf Giant

Anita Lobel

A Mulberry Paperback Book New York

The Library of Congress has cataloged the
Greenwillow Books edition of *The Dwarf Giant* as follows:
Lobel, Anita. The dwarf giant / by Anita Lobel   p.   cm.
Summary: Prince Mainichi and Princess Ichinichi
are visited by a rude dwarf, who inflicts upon them
evil and dangerous games before revealing his true self.
ISBN 0-688-14407-1
[1. Fairy tales. 2. Dwarfs—Fiction. 3. Japan—Fiction.]
I. Title. PZ8.L775Dw 1996 [E]—dc20
95-6790 CIP AC

1 3 5 7 9 10 8 6 4 2
First Mulberry Edition, 1996
ISBN 0-688-14408-X

For my good friend
Allan Manning, with love

Long, long ago, beyond the ocean, on the other side of the world, there was a quiet and peaceful country where an elegant palace stood on top of a hill.

In the palace lived the handsome prince Mainichi and his beautiful princess Ichinichi.

The people of the land worked very hard. They loved their prince and princess. The sun shone, the moon sailed across the sky, and every day was much like every other.

One evening Prince Mainichi and Princess Ichinichi were looking at the moon shining over the ocean.

"How beautiful it is," sighed the princess.

"Yes," murmured the prince. "Just like all the other evenings. Sometimes I wish something new and exciting would happen to me."

Just then a small boat with battered sails appeared on the horizon. Swiftly it drifted to shore.

A dwarf stepped out and walked up the hill.
"I was caught in a storm at sea," said the little
man. "May I visit for a while?"
"You are most welcome in our quiet and peaceful
country," said Princess Ichinichi.
"We seldom have guests," said Prince Mainichi.
"Please share our evening meal."
The dwarf quickly gobbled up the rice rolls,
mushrooms, and chicken cutlets with ginger
and mustard.

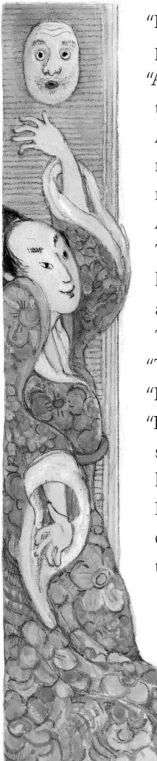

"Please dance for our honored guest," said the prince to the princess.

"Allow *me* to play for you tonight instead," said the dwarf. He picked up the prince's flute. As soon as the dwarf began to play, a little mouse danced on the tip of the flute. The mouse vanished as quickly as it had appeared. A small snake coiled itself around the flute. The flute grew bigger as the music grew louder. The snake vanished and an owl appeared. The music grew even louder. The owl hooted and flew away.

"This is magic!" exclaimed the prince.

"I'm frightened," whispered the princess.

"Don't be," said the prince. "Finally something exciting is happening in our kingdom."

Next the flute changed into a drum. The dwarf beat on it until it sounded like roaring thunder.

"Now dance!" the dwarf yelled over the drumbeats.
The prince grabbed the princess and began to twirl
and spin her around and around.
"All of you dance!" shouted the dwarf to the servants.
"Dance to my music!"
The palace shook and trembled as everyone danced.

But far away, at the very edge of the land, an old farmer awoke from a dream. "Listen," he said, waking his wife. The farmer and his wife were frightened by the strange sounds. They could not go back to sleep.

At the palace, when the sun began to rise, the dwarf stopped playing. The tired servants fell into a deep sleep. The drum had changed into a flute again. The dwarf returned it to the dazed prince.

"This palace is a shambles!" exclaimed the princess.

"Never mind." Her husband laughed. "I am having fun."

"If you follow me, you can have still more fun," said the dwarf.

He skipped to the biggest cherry tree in the garden and climbed to the top. The prince climbed after him. Branches began to crack and break off.

"You are ruining our beautiful cherry tree!" the princess cried out. "Stop it at once!"

"You are being very rude to my good friend!" shouted the prince.

The dwarf shook the tree violently. Cherry blossoms turned to pebbles and fell down on the princess.

"Stop him!" the princess pleaded. "He's bad. He will hurt us!"

"Get rid of that silly woman," said the dwarf to the prince. "You can dance and play all you want with me."

The dwarf jumped down from the cherry tree.

"Wait for me," cried the prince. Together they danced off, trampling the flower beds.

"Come to your senses, husband!" begged the princess. "Stop these evil games!"

"Games!" the dwarf mumbled. "I will show you a game!"

He waved his arms, and a chessboard appeared. The chess
pieces jumped off the board and chased the princess away.
"At last she is gone, my dear friend!" The prince giggled.
"Now we can play and have fun by ourselves!"

The princess ran from the palace. She ran and ran until she came to the house where the old farmer and his wife lived.

"I must save my husband and my home from an evil dwarf," cried the princess.

"We want to help," said the farmer's wife.

After they drank some tea together, the princess said, "Come with me. I have thought of a plan."

At the palace the prince and the dwarf were now jumping up and down, poking the sleeping servants. "Wake up! Wake up!" yelled the prince. "It's time to have a party. My best friend will show you some wonderful magic tricks."

The dwarf did a somersault, and a large
rat dangled from the prince's ear. The
prince giggled. The rat vanished, and
a big snake coiled around the prince's
waist. The prince began to tremble with
fear. The snake changed into a large bat
that landed on the prince's head.

"Stop! Stop!" the prince cried. "I don't like
these games anymore."

The dwarf did a double somersault and turned
into a giant holding a burning sword.

"Now you do some tricks for me!" yelled the
dwarf giant. "Swallow the sword."

"I can't," sobbed the prince. "Let's play as we
did before, my friend."

"You silly fool. I have never been your friend!"
the dwarf giant roared. "I have come to
destroy you and take over your kingdom."

Just then another giant appeared. This giant had
many arms. Each arm held a sword.

"You do not frighten me!" the dwarf giant shouted.
"I can grow ten times bigger than you. I can swallow a tiny
giant like you in one gulp."

The dwarf giant took a hissing breath. He puffed himself
up, growing bigger and bigger.

There was a loud rumbling sound, and the dwarf giant burst into a thousand pieces. The palace trembled. The whole country shook.

"The evil giant is gone," whispered the people in amazement. "The spell is broken!"

Prince Mainichi fell on his knees
before the good, many-armed giant.
"Thank you for saving my life,
wonderful creature, whoever you are,"
he sobbed.
"Stop crying, you foolish man!"
Princess Ichinichi said.
The disguised farmers lifted her down
from their shoulders.
"Thank you, my good friends," said
the princess. "You were very strong
and very brave."
"My dearest wife," said the prince,
"please forgive me for having been such
a fool. My dear people, help me repair
what was trampled and broken. Then
let us celebrate."

The palace was made beautiful once more. The lanterns were lit, and people came from all over the kingdom. A great feast of many delicious foods was served. The prince played wonderful music on his flute, and the princess danced. Everyone was happy.

At last the prince and princess lay down to sleep.
Later that night a servant appeared and whispered,
"Someone is knocking at the gate, Your Highness!"
"What shall we do?" Princess Ichinichi asked.
"Let's look at the moon for now," said Prince Mainichi.
"We will think about what to do tomorrow."

E   Lobel, Anita.
LOB   The dwarf giant

DATE DUE			